W9-CFO-045

Bernie Entertaining

Also by Larry Bograd

POOR GERTIE
THE KOLOKOL PAPERS

Bernie
Entertaining

Larry Bograd

ILLUSTRATED BY RICHARD LAUTER

DELACORTE PRESS/NEW YORK

ELLETTSVILLE ELEMENTARY LIBRARY

Published by
Delacorte Press
1 Dag Hammarskjold Plaza
New York, New York 10017

F
BOG
c . 1

Text copyright © 1987 by Larry Bograd
Illustrations copyright © 1987 by Richard Lauter

3 -88 Baker + Taylor ᵴ 12 -95

All rights reserved. No part of this book may be reproduced or transmitted in
any form or by any means, electronic or mechanical, including photocopying,
recording or by any information storage and retrieval system, without the
written permission of the Publisher, except where permitted by law.

Library of Congress Cataloging-in-Publication Data
Bograd, Larry.
Bernie entertaining.
Summary: Ten-year-old Bernie's comic misadventures
at home and school do not seem very humorous to him,
reinforcing his terrible self-image and convincing him
that he will never succeed at anything important.
[1. Self-perception—Fiction. 2. Family life—
Fiction. 3. Schools—Fiction. 4. Humorous stories]
I. Lauter, Richard, ill. II. Title.
PZ7.B635784Be 1987   [Fic]   86-19633
ISBN 0-385-29543-X

Manufactured in the United States of America

First printing

For Jeffrey Robinson

Bernie
Entertaining

1

Call me Bernie.

All truly famous people only need one name. Like Superman and Bozo.

My real name is Bernard, which I hate. What were my parents thinking when they picked out that name? Did they want to punish me?—I wasn't born yet! They should've waited and asked me my choice. I'd have chosen an astronaut's name. Like Bim or Buzz or Gordo. Bernard is a name for a nerd, not an astronaut.

People think I'm a nerd because I like science and hate sports. Because I prefer screens to screams. Plus I was one of the first kids in my class to get glasses. Glasses magnify the brain, you know.

The only time I'm not a nerd is at night. Nighttime is the right time. After Mom, Dad, and my older sister Lisa go to bed, I sneak out of my room. Mom can't scream at me while she sleeps. Dad has a decent reason to ignore me —he's in dreamland. Lisa sleeps without moving. She doesn't want to smear her zit medicine. So the house is mine.

Our wall-to-wall carpet feels oily against my stomach as I elbow myself forward. Low below our burglar alarm laser beam. My eyes are electronic scouts. I scan for furniture. I spot Cecil, our dog, who was born before me. Cecil lived with Mom before Dad did. Mom wouldn't have married Dad if Cecil hadn't approved. Luckily for Lisa and me, Cecil liked Dad. Now Cecil's too old to do much other than sleep and eat. Lying on his side, he wags his tail and winks at me.

Crawling, I reach our kitchen. I brake too hard—and the slick floor joyrides me into a crash landing against our fridge. I moan, fall on my back, and look up.

I can hear our neighbor's electric bugkiller zapping pests. I'm afraid that I woke Mom and she'll phone the police. Or Dad will find his glasses and gun. He owns a Magnum like Clint Eastwood does. I lie still, awaiting my fate.

Luckily, nothing happens. I'm invisible. I roll over and slide toward our back door. There I snake up a wall and punch out the Disarm code on our security system. Now it's safe to go outside, which Mom and Dad think is unsafe.

I unlock and slide open our patio door. Air! The night sky! Freedom!

Down on all fours so the neighbors won't shoot me, I crawl across our cold, damp lawn. "Next time, genius," I tell myself, "remember your gloves and kneepads!" In the center of our yard I lie on my back and look up. The gray sky is loaded with stars! Pinpoints of white. Other worlds. I find the constellations I know. The Big and Little Dippers. Orion the Hunter. Pegasus the Flying Horse.

How I wish I could fly. To float in the sky! To be surrounded by endless space! I'd drop in on alien friends. I'd
watch over the world, not waking anybody. I'd observe
the bad guys, ready to sound the alarm. I'd whisper into
drunks' ears that they shouldn't drive. I'd show missing
children home. I'd collect all the cancer in a special jar
and hurl it away. I'd contact Einstein's brain and then find
Robert Goddard, Father of American Rocketry. I'd circle
the moon and be home for breakfast. No one would have
to know.

In space I wouldn't worry if I'm popular. I'd do as I
pleased, all choices mine. Sing as loud as I want. Being
weightless, I'd be as strong as any jock.

I stare at the sky till my eyes start to water. I chant, "Fall
into the sky. Fall into the sky. . . ." I try to lift off from our
lawn. For a moment I think it's working. That I'm lifting
off. That the mission computer has started Elapsed Time.
That I'll sneak through our Star Wars System and wave
good-bye to sorry old earth.

Then I become scared. What if it works this time? What
if I'm actually hovering above our lawn? What if a UFO
tractor beam catches me and takes me away forever? Or I
drift, lost in space? What if the White House fears I'm a
terrorist? I'll be blasted out of the sky! What if a rifleman
mistakes me for a goose? Or a goose mistakes me for
another goose?

Maybe it's better to be earthbound. For this night, at
least. I feel the ground about me—and I'm relieved.
Maybe one day NASA will select me as an astronaut. I

have to come up with a plan. A way that NASA will notice me. A way to become famous.

I lie there. And I can't think of anything. It's hard to think with a cold tush. So I go back inside and try to sleep.

With luck, the sky will be there tomorrow night.

2

I haven't been in a hospital since the day I was born. I have no bad habits. I can follow directions. And I love my country. All in all, I'm a perfect candidate for the space program. For this reason, I *had* to stay home from school last week. And I had to be *really* sick, since I'd faked it the week before. Luckily, I had the perfect plan.

Step one: I had to wake up before my parents did.

So the night before the night before, after saying "Good night! Sleep tight! I lo-o-o-o-o-ove you!" I closed my door and opened my curtains and window. A cool breeze floated in to keep me company. I fell asleep watching the stars and feeling the night's breeze. I dreamed of flying to the polar cap. Seeing my science teacher frozen stiff. Being on TV with my own show. Teaching the polar bears the boogaloo. Painting my igloo blue. And I woke up to the sound of garbage trucks, the sun's glare in my eyes.

Step two: Outsmarting them. I had to make my parents believe I was really ill.

After carefully removing myself from bed, I jumped to my feet. (I sleep without moving and never have to make my bed in the morning. I'm very proud of it.) I ran in place for five minutes then ran to the bathroom. I misted myself with warm water and put baby oil all through my hair. I checked my appearance in the mirror: not looking sad enough, I poked myself in the eyes and ran out.

I stopped outside their door to make certain they were asleep. I didn't want to barge in and see something weird. All I heard was Dad's snoring. Good—he'd sleep through the whole scene.

I opened the door and crept inside, not wanting Mom to see me before I was ready.

There she lay. Sound asleep. At my mercy! I was so excited I nearly tumbled on top of her.

Silently I extended my hand toward her body. The tips of my fingers vibrated and my heart was pounding. I leaned my head forward, my lips going straight for her cheek. Mom looked so peaceful.

I took one last breath deep into my lungs. Then I exhaled, trapping the air as it approached the top of my throat. I held it there for one second as I ran the checklist through my brain to make sure I had thought of everything.

Her face was soft and puffy. Her tongue touched her bottom lip. A lock of hair shielded her eyes. She was all mine.

"MO-O-OM-M-M!" I moaned as loudly as I could. "I don't feel so well!"

Her eyelids clamped down. Her brain was confused. She couldn't believe it. My fingers landed on her shoulder. I started to pump up and down. The mattress creaked.

"Mommmmm!" I whispered. "I'm sick, Mom. Really sick. I think I'm running a fever. I'm hot. I'd better stay home. I'm sick." I spoke quickly, hoping to overload her brain.

For starters, she knew who I was. "Bernie," she said, sounding fuzzy, "did you have an accident? Should we talk about it or just change the sheets?"

"Oh, Mom! *That* hasn't happened in five years!"

She raised her head from the pillow, keeping her neck stiff. "Bernie, aren't you feeling well?"

"No. . . . I mean yes. I mean . . . I'm burning up, Mom. I'm sick as a dog. Maybe sicker."

As she sat up, her arms reached for me. She had me in a headlock before I could do anything. "Let me feel you."

Then I remembered that I had forgotten to warm my forehead!

"You don't feel warm to me, Bernie." She checked several spots on my brow. "You don't have a temperature."

"But, Mom . . ." I had to stay on my toes. "My pajamas are soaking. The fever's gone from my head. It's settled in my chest, and my lungs are boiling."

Mom sat back. She wasn't sure, so she tried to wake Dad. "Honey, can a fever go from the head to the chest?" She was poking him with her knee.

Dad rolled over. He sighed, kept his eyes closed. "What's the problem?" I saw his bald spot, which he tries to cover when awake.

"Bernie has something. He can't sleep. He's never up this early, so he must be sick."

Great! I had them in my clutches!

"Have you taken his temperature?" Dad asked.

"I'm hot, Dad. Really hot," I said in a direct appeal.

He rubbed the night's whiskers. "Hmmmm. What will you do at school today, son? Anything important?"

I had a ready answer. "No, nothing important. We had a math test yesterday. We won't start a new science chapter until next Monday, so I won't miss a thing."

Dad opened one eye and looked up at Mom. "Why don't we let him stay home? It's probably nothing. Let's stay on the safe side. We can't afford to run up any doctors' bills."

"Okay." Mom turned to me. "Bernie, get right back into bed. I'll bring you some juice." I started to leave. "And put another blanket on your bed."

"Can I use the electric blanket?" I asked.

"No, the bill's already too high."

I looked at her and conceded a small point. "Okay, Mom. Whatever you say." Turning and hiding a smile, I shuffled to the door. Sunlight shone down the hallway. In my room I flung up my arms in victory. Home for the day! I'd be the only kid—except for the *really* sick ones—who could watch the new, improved space shuttle blast-off on TV.

I pranced around my room, singing the theme song of my hit TV show:

> *Look at him. He's such a groovy guy.*
> *That's our Bim. Watch how he flies.*
> *Our Space Ranger in danger!*
> *Our Number One in the sky.*

"For we know, nothing is stranger"
Is our motto cry.

Then my announcer, a part-time bass with the opera, would come on: *"Space Ranger* is brought to you by our star—Bim!"

The screen would flash my best-selling poster: me dressed in an aluminum tuxedo.

I'm such a big star that all the commercials would be for my movies—*Bim. The Movie; Bim II; Bim and the Return of the Lord;* and *Bim Does Dallas*—and my books—*Bim: By Bim, Why Bim?* and the gigantic best seller *100 Uses for Bim.*

And to top it off—Mom was bringing in a glass of cold orange juice.

It had been a perfect day and the sun was barely up.

Mom and Dad left, dragging Lisa with them. Lisa was convinced I was faking and told my parents so. She was upset because *she* hadn't thought of a better plan.

By 9:05, when all my friends were pledging allegiance, I was back asleep. Dreaming of falling into the sky. Waving to the space shuttle. Washing its windows. Checking its oil. Gluing *Space Ranger* decals to its wings.

Waking at 10:14, I had plenty of time to use the bathroom and find my glasses and get dressed and grab my blanket and run down the hall to the TV.

I turned the set on and couldn't decide which of the ninety channels to choose. So I tried my favorite number, and sure enough, they were at the launch. They had the best programming!

I settled down on the floor and pulled the blanket around Cecil and me. No sooner were we comfy, when I heard some horrible news.

There had to be a mistake. I couldn't believe it. I tried several other channels, but the story remained the same. I turned up the sound.

At mission control a reporter asked the flight director, "Does this mean you'll delay the mission?"

"We're still studying the data," he answered. "By that I mean our computers are running through their functions."

"And what does that mean?" No one had understood his answer.

"We have a decision-making process here at the space agency," the flight director said. "The Go–No Go is not the decision of just one person. But we'll make a decision by . . . oh, say . . . 10:42."

There were four minutes to wait. The channel broke for commercials. Tropical fruits danced along a Hawaiian shore. A car complained about its bad muffler. A guy tried to sell me a home computer that did everything but walk the dog. A bunch of teenagers ran down a beach, ripped off their clothes, and drank cola. A woman soaked her fingers in dishwashing soap. Finally, the Cape Canaveral announcer came on with the important stuff. "We have just heard from mission control. The launch has been postponed until tomorrow."

Postponed! On my day home from school? If I pretended I was sick tomorrow, my parents would trade me in. Life was so unfair!

I rolled on my back and kicked the blanket from my legs. Cecil ran and hid. I had the whole boring day in front of me.

When I stopped being mad, I understood that NASA was right to postpone the lift-off. Ever since the *Challenger* shuttle blew up, people had to be extra careful.

I remembered that horrible day. After it happened, I felt like someone in my family had died. I felt so bad that I wrote NASA a letter, saying how sorry I felt for the dead astronauts' families. For a long time after, I didn't want to become an astronaut myself.

Of course, people die all the time. But seeing the *Challenger* blow up was so unexpected. A shock. I guess so much success and good luck had made lots of people, including me, believe nothing would ever go wrong. Maybe the government shouldn't have sent that teacher, Christa McAuliffe, into space, since space travel isn't all that safe yet.

Lisa, who likes to be negative, thinks the government used Ms. McAuliffe to disguise the fact that NASA is sending all sorts of military stuff into orbit. That the teacher-in-space program was a publicity stunt—after all, there's plenty of people and problems on earth who need attention. There's poor people without proper food or shelter, for instance. As much as I like the space program, I have to admit that Lisa was right. But what was one kid to do?

After a lot of thought, I wrote the President this letter:

Dear Mr. President,

Sorry about what happened to the *Challenger*. Maybe you should learn that no machine is perfect. That space should be left to dreamers. Maybe you should make no more weapons or, at least, not send them into space.

Yours truly,
Bernie

The White House sent me a note, thanking me for my letter. The note was signed by a machine that copied the President's signature.

3

Dad was rich as a kid. Dad's father had invented the dog biscuit. When Dad was a teenager his family lost all their money. Dad's dad tried to sell cat biscuits. They were a big flop. Cats, you know, have too much pride to beg or play dead.

Mom's family was poor. Her father went broke trying to introduce sushi into the United States. Mom says Grandpa was ahead of his time, and Grandpa agrees. He told me on the phone, "Bernard, I should be a billionaire owning a baseball team. I knew sushi would be a hit. But I opened my restaurant in 1943, during World War Two. Mobs tried to burn it down."

"I wish you were rich too," I told him to make him happy. He and Grandma live in Florida. Dad's parents are both dead. They didn't stick around to meet me.

Mom wanted to be an artist, but she went to college and married Dad instead. Cecil was Best Dog at their wedding. Now Mom works at the art museum, raising money to buy paintings. The best paintings are by dead artists.

And the more dead the artist is, the more expensive the painting.

Dad wanted to be surrounded by money all his life. So he works in a bank. He's worked there for fifteen years.

Lisa was born first. She's two years older than me and now she's "suffering puberty," as Mom puts it. All of a sudden, Lisa thinks breasts are the most important thing in the world.

While waiting for breasts, Lisa keeps busy after school with music and dance and gymnastics lessons. With Mom and Dad at work, I'm alone most afternoons. Not that I mind—I watch TV or read. Lately I've been working my way through our encyclopedia. I take a volume down each day and leaf through it. With twenty volumes it works out perfectly—I can go through the encyclopedia every month.

I should get better grades, but I get marked down for bad penmanship. Or the tests are too hard. Or the homework too boring. Dad says I have to get good grades if I want to become an astronaut. I tell him I want to become an astronaut whether my grades are good or not. Dad says I need more discipline and should try sports. "Just because you're the smallest kid in your class doesn't mean you can't be a top jock," he says. I thank him, go to my room, and look at the pictures of the moon, planets, and stars that I've taped to my wall.

Out my window I can see another new house being built down our block. Last year we were surrounded by vacant lots. Fields of wild grass and rabbits. I used to hunt for dinosaur bones or arrowheads. Now we're surrounded

by smelly barbecues and loud lawn mowers. Dad calls this
"progress."

Lisa's best friend, Erin, used to live across the street. I
liked Erin. Her house had the best video games on the
block. Whenever she came over she said hello to me.

One day I overheard them in Lisa's room.

"Promise me you'll never get married," Erin was telling Lisa. "Swear on our oath as sisters."

"I swear. What happened?"

"Promise we'll meet in Paris in ten years and live together till we die."

"I promise. Erin! Tell me what happened?"

"Swear we'll never listen to men. We'll do what *we* like
when we want to. Promise me, Lisa."

I heard my sister say to Erin, "Spill the beans!"

It was quiet for a moment. "Dad left us last night," Erin
said. "He walked off. Mom called a lawyer this morning.
My parents are getting a divorce!"

"Why?"

"Because they don't get along," Erin said. "They don't
hate each other, nothing like that. They say the marriage
was a mistake. If the marriage was a mistake, what does
that make me?"

Then she started to cry. Lisa started to cry too, and I
wasn't very thrilled myself. Erin was a good person. She
hadn't done anything wrong. Now her life was as mixed
up as her parents'.

They sold the house, and Erin moved away to Florida
with her mother. A judge had to decide who got the video
games. Lisa's been a wreck ever since. She mopes around

the house. She writes Erin every day and gets to phone her once a month. I tell Lisa that Erin should visit Grandpa and Grandma. Lisa tells me to "mind my own beeswax!"

At dinner she stares at our parents. "Are you getting a divorce?" she asks them. "It's the latest fad. Go on. Dad, you can take Bernie, and I'll live with Mom."

"Fine with me," I announce.

"Bernard, lock that mouth!" Dad snarls.

Mom looks at Lisa. "Is something wrong with the food? Is that why you're upset?"

My sister is skating on thin ice. She could get *me* into trouble if she upsets Mom and Dad too much. Dinner *is* bad: some horrible frozen chicken-and-nuts meals that Mom bought at the store. They were more expensive than pizza, which is always my first choice.

"Lisa, we're not getting a divorce," Dad tells her, touching her arm. "Mom and I love each other, in spite of you kids."

Mom tells Dad, "This is no time to joke, dear."

"I'm sorry," Dad tells us. "Lisa, are you sad because Erin left?"

"What do *you* think?" Lisa asks.

Dad leans back and thinks about it. "I think, yes, you're upset because Erin moved away."

"Good guess, Sherlock!" Lisa says.

"Mom, I want to be an astronaut," I declare, changing the subject before Lisa gets us into trouble.

My parents look at me. "Bernie, we'll talk about you

later, okay?" Mom says. "Lisa is trying to tell us something."

"No, I'm not," Lisa shouts. "I want to eat dinner alone from now on!"

"We'll talk about *that* after we finish *this,*" Dad says, putting his foot down.

"Since Bernard is so eager," Lisa says, "let him hog the spotlight."

"Lisa, we'll talk later, okay?" Mom says quietly. They have an alliance—Mom and Lisa. They wake me at night with their whispering. They meet in the bathroom! Mom takes a hot bath and Lisa . . . well, watches. And they talk.

"May I go to my room now? I'm not hungry," Lisa says.

"Stay here, young lady, and finish your food," Dad orders. "Children are starving in Africa."

"Then send the food to them. They'd *have* to be starving to eat this stuff!"

"Let her go," Mom tells Dad.

Lisa leaves the table. We hear her door slam shut. Mom shrugs her shoulders. Dad shrugs his shoulders. I shrug mine.

"You should take us to Florida," I suggest. "That would make Lisa feel better. She could visit Erin, and I could visit Cape Canaveral. We can stay with Grandpa and Grandma and save money."

"Son, money doesn't grow on trees," Dad says. "We can't afford the airfare."

"You and Mom could sit on the beach. Dad, you could go deep-sea fishing. We can visit Disney World!"

"Bernie, we don't have the money," Mom tells me.

"We could hitchhike."

"Bernie, drop it."

"We could get on TV and ask for donations."

"Bernard!"

"I just want to see the space shuttle blast off, that's all."

"You can watch it on TV," Mom says.

"It's not the same thing. The living room doesn't shake."

"Become president first," Dad says. "Then you could appoint yourself to NASA." He winks at Mom.

"How do I become president?"

"You have to have plenty of time and money."

"How do I get plenty of money?" I ask.

Dad smiles. "You have to become a famous athlete. Work hard in gym. Then, in high school, try out for the football team. College scouts will watch you play. If you're good, you'll be signed by the pros for millions of dollars."

"What happens if I break my glasses in gym?" I ask.

"You'll have a hard time focusing," Dad says. What a barrel of laughs he is!

Mom stands and starts to clear the table. This only gives me two minutes before she reminds me it's my night to help her. Which means I stand in the kitchen and repeat "Now what should I do? Now what should I do?" till she has had enough and lets me go.

I wait for her to leave. She'll put the dishes in the sink to soak, then she'll call her friend Dr. Skizz and talk about Lisa. Lisa gets all the attention around here. She's older.

She's the only girl. She's suffering puberty. She and Mom are both female. Good thing Dad's around.

"If I become president, can I really appoint myself an astronaut?" I ask Dad.

"Bernie, some people become astronauts, then try to become president. Remember John Glenn?"

"Sure. He was the first American to orbit the earth."

"Right, and he once ran for president. President Reagan was a movie actor and sportscaster. President Ford was a football player in his day. A lot of athletes end up in politics." Dad is full of useless information.

"Okay, I'll try it," I tell him. Dad always bugs me about sports. He thinks sports build character. "I'll make you proud," I tell him.

4

The most famous kid in school is my neighbor James James. His parents named him that just to get him on the TV news. They wanted to give him a head start. James James is perfect. He's handsome and a top jock. His grades are good enough and he doesn't choke on his food. He and his dad are like brothers.

I know my dad loves me—and that he'd love me more if I was a jock. Dad was quite a jock in his day. He doesn't care about space travel. He cares about Mom, money, Lisa, the St. Louis Cardinals, and me.

I'd like to make Dad proud, but sports scare me. Baseballs are hard and fast. Footballs are big and pointed. I thought about talking with Mom, but she's Lisa's ally. No, I'd have to try it Dad's way.

I tell James James in gym I want to join his after-school football league. He has just kicked a ball to put his team way ahead. I hadn't felt like playing, so I'm one of the goalposts.

"Be at the park at four o'clock," he tells me, trotting away. "Ready to play. Ready to kill!"

I arrive at the park to see boys fighting, tripping one another, and throwing hunks of earth. They're banging and knocking and poking one another. I ask James James what's going on.

"We're just warming up," he tells me.

Then the equipment arrives: hard rubber balls that are impossible to grip, padded elbow and knee braces, helmets, whistles. The boys start fighting over the gear.

Then the coach, Attila the Hun, shows up. "All right, you flabby pansies! I've seen tougher meat on my plate! You're soft. Slow and soft and ugly! You're not winners— you're weiners! Get out of my sight before I puke! Run— and you'd better run!—to the fence and back five times. If I catch any of you slime loafing, I'll have your rump!"

The rest of the boys take off.

I walk up to the coach. "Excuse me," I say, "but I'd like to—"

He looks down and snarls, "What are you doing?"

"I'm trying to explain. I . . ."

"Do you want to be a ballplayer?" he bellows.

"Yes, very soon." I smile. "James James is my friend. And . . ."

"I don't care if you're Walter Payton's son! Get out of my sight! Take off!"

"What?"

"You're behind the others. Run! A ballplayer has got to have legs!"

I look down. "I have mine."

He lifts me and throws me toward the fence. I get the idea. I start to chase the others.

I nearly catch up to them, when they hit the fence and face me. I'm caught in a stampede!

I try to dodge Bronto Blahberg. He's the biggest kid in my class. He's also a bully, so he belts me. I go sailing, land on my shoulder, and roll over. My glasses ram against my knee.

Looking up, I see cleats the size of beds, ready to trample me. I protect my skull.

When the ground begins to rumble, I know I'm a goner. I can see the headlines:

BIM IS BEDRIDDEN!
CLEAT COMPANY IS SUED!

I roll my body into a ball, and somehow my life is spared.

When I stand up, I find green blotches on my arms and blood on my hands.

The rumbling starts anew. I look up to see them charging toward me, their heads low, their teeth bared. I leap for the sidelines and barely make it.

I go over to the coach for an explanation. "I nearly got killed," I say. "How are you going to have a team if everyone dies in practice?"

He's biting his nails. "What are you doing here?"

I wasn't so sure myself.

He gives me the once-over. "Kid," he tells me, "I've been coaching for years. I've never seen a boy like you."

"Thank you," I reply.

He shakes his fist. "I'd like to meet your parents. I'd give them a piece of my mind."

He didn't seem to have that much to spare.

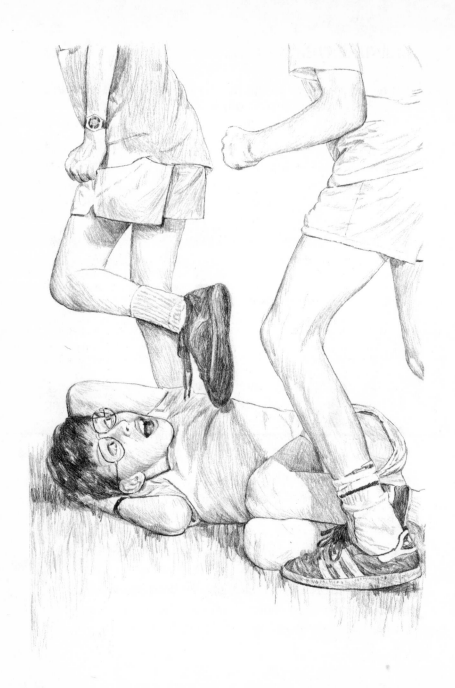

The boys, led by James James, arrive and surround us. James is barely winded. He's such a jock!

"What are we going to do on Saturday?" the coach asks.

"WIN!" they all shout.

"How are we going to do it?"

"We'll fight! We'll kick 'em. Kick 'em where the sun don't shine!"

"How many times?" bellows the coach.

"All game long!"

"Until?" The coach and the boys are jumping like pogo sticks.

"Until they cry for their mommies!"

"And then?" the coach screams. His face is as red as a valentine.

"We'll kick 'em some more!" The boys fall to the ground and start to rip the turf.

Attila the Hun looks at me. "Listen, squirt, you can be trainer."

"Trainer? What good is that? The trainer only runs onto the field during commercials. Maybe football isn't for me," I say, walking off.

No one runs after me, telling me to change my mind. I'm a wimp. A failure. I feel like a real Bernard, and nothing's lower. Will I be a nobody for all time? Last in war? Last in peace? Last in the hearts of my classmates? A nobody? A zero?

Nobody cares about you if you're not a someone. Only someones get anywhere. Only someones get rocketed into space and drink Tang.

5

We're almost through dinner when Dad asks, "How was football?"

I glance at Mom and Lisa, hoping they'll quickly change the subject, since they hate sports. But they're waiting for my answer too.

I roll up my sleeve and show Dad how puny my arm is. "Football's not for me. I nearly got killed today!"

"Bernie, America doesn't like quitters," Dad says.

I shrug. "Then America hates me."

Dad gives Mom one of his "How did us good folks end up with such a worthless kid?" looks.

I have to come up with something quickly, or lose Dad as an ally forever. "Would you rather I was a top jock or a top student?" I ask.

"A top student," Mom answers first, knowing it'd be a hard choice for Dad.

"Then I'll work harder in school," I say, trapped. "We're having a special report on family heritage next week. If I get an A, I'll get an A for the grading period."

"Bernard," Lisa sneers, "you wouldn't know an A if it bit you on the lip."

I lean across the table, close to her face. "Why, Lisa! Is that a zit I see on your forehead?"

"Where?" she demands.

"Bernie," Mom warns.

But I'm in too deep to stop. "There," I say, pointing to Lisa's head. "Oh, it's so big. Maybe your breasts are growing in a weird place!"

In a flash Lisa runs crying from the table; Mom glares at me, then chases after her; Dad rolls his eyes, wipes his mouth, and tosses his napkin down. My ears are burning—I'm in trouble now!

"Son—" Dad starts.

"Yeah, I know. 'Go to your room and stew in your own juices.'" I take my dishes to the sink, then go to my room. There I can hear Mom and Lisa talking in the next room. Everyone's mad at me—and just because Dad forced me to get trampled at football.

Why can't I be someone else? Why couldn't I have been born James James? He's an only child. He lives in a ten-bedroom house, with a color TV in every room and a satellite dish in the front yard.

One night James slept over. We talked about sports, of course. Suddenly he screamed, "I got to watch TV!" His eyes bulged. He shivered. He was about to pass out.

"Does this happen often?" I asked him.

"Bernie, no fooling. Oklahoma is playing Oklahoma

State on cable TV! If I don't watch the game, Dad will kill me!"

"Try to relax," I told him. We had a problem. Mom and Dad had canceled cable TV. They said it showed too many X-rated movies.

James was desperate. "Where's the TV? Do you want me to die?"

"No, if you die, I won't have any friends," I said. "We don't have cable TV. But it's still light. Let's bike to the mall."

"You don't have cable TV!" James was amazed. "If my house didn't have cable TV, Dad would never come home."

We biked to the mall, bought Orange Juliuses, and stood outside the electronics store. The game was on twelve different sets inside. At the same instant, twelve Oklahoma quarterbacks threw twelve footballs to twelve receivers, who scored twelve touchdowns.

I did a quick calculation. "That's seventy-two points."

"Great!" James smiled. "Oklahoma is killing State. Dad will be thrilled. We can go now."

We biked back to my house. Mom and Dad weren't home yet. Lisa was using the living room as her private study. Her books were all over the couch. The TV and stereo were off. No picture. No noise. I led James to my room.

"Can't we talk to Lisa?" he asked.

"*You* might be able to," I said. "She won't talk to me. We're fighting."

"What are you fighting about?"

I had to think for a moment. "This time, it's the bath-room. I forget to put the toilet seat down. And Lisa *claims* she nearly fell in. Either she goes to the bathroom in the dark, or she has the world's smallest tushy."

"What did you fight about before that?" James asked, suddenly a reporter on *Sixty Minutes.*

"Caffeine-free sodas. Lisa wants Mom to buy them, but I'm against the idea. I like my soda as nature meant me to drink it."

"I wish I had a sister," he told me. "Dad thinks he's my older brother, but I know he's my father. I wish I had a sister."

"Make me an offer," I said, "and I'll talk to my parents."

"I'm serious, Bernie."

"So am I."

"Why do you and Lisa fight?"

"Why?" I looked at him. I had to think for a moment again.

"Well," I said, "she's my sister and a girl, for starters. She and Mom are good buddies, and Dad mostly worries about money. Sometimes he says he's going to take me on a trip, just the two of us. But he hasn't done anything yet. So that leaves me without much to do except bother Lisa. It's easy to bother her nowadays because she's already upset that Erin left."

"Maybe you should be more understanding," James said.

"Isn't that what parents are for?" I asked. "I mean, Mom is understanding—about Lisa. But Dad doesn't see that Lisa's upset, which steams her. So she turns on me to get back at him. And we go round and round. Now can I show you my space collection?" I opened my folder of astronaut photos.

"One day there'll be Space Olympics," James predicted. "Someone will hurl a shotput that will travel around the cosmos and hit him in the back of the head."

"James, you should design video games," I said, paying him the highest praise.

"What do you like about space?" he asked.

"It's not *here,*" I told him. "Up there, in space, earth is a speck in a vast nothingness." I turn off the lights.

"'A speck in a vast nothingness,'" James repeated. "Gosh, that's a depressing thought."

"It doesn't have to be. I don't exist in space. I'm too small. There are billions and billions of stars that are a billion times bigger than me."

"You're making me sad," James said. "You mean no one in space knows me?"

"I'm afraid not," I told him. "Now, can I ask *you* a question? Do you dream?"

"Yes."

"Do you ever dream that you're flying?"

"Flying *where?*"

"Not *where?*" I said. "Flying free."

"Like a dragonfly?" he asked.

"Higher," I said, flapping my arms.

"Like a kicked football?"

"Higher, James."

"Like an eagle?"

"Forget it," I said. "You don't dream of flying. What *do* you dream about?"

He closed his eyes and thought. "I dream that a gigantic praying mantis picks up our station wagon and tries to eat us."

"Do you get away—in the dream?" I asked.

"Yes. I fall out of a window and crash to the ground. I get up and start to run for help, but there's no one to run to. Mom and Dad are trapped in the car. The bug's about to chew them apart. I scream. . . . Then I wake up and eat a full breakfast."

"Wow." I wondered what a praying mantis prays for.

"Lisa must have more friends than just Erin," he said.

"No. She has Erin and I have you. It's not easy making friends," I told him.

"I wouldn't know. I've always been popular. Mom tells me I should become a soap opera star. Dad, of course, expects me to become an all-American football star."

"How did you become popular?" I asked him. "What's the secret?"

He shrugged his shoulders. "Guess you either have it or you don't. Guess I was born special."

"Well, everyone thought Einstein was an idiot when he was a kid, and look how he turned out," I told him.

"He died," James said.

"True, but before that the world realized he was a genius."

James smirked. "Oh, and you're going to grow up to be another Einstein? Don't make me laugh!"

"People told Robert Goddard that his rocket experiments were a waste—and he finally succeeded."

"Who's Robert Goddard?"

"The father of American rocketry, that's what the encyclopedia says," I informed him.

"Well, I've never heard of him, so he can't be famous," James said. He stared at me. "What are *you* going to do to become famous?" he asked.

"Wait and see," I said.

He smirked again. "Right. Wait and see how big a fool you make of yourself!"

If I were twice his size, I would've belted him! I put my astronaut photos back in their folder. "Wait and see," I repeated.

6

James James has football practice, so I'm home, all alone. It's all right. I think Lisa has gone to the mall or, if I am lucky, has taken the bus to the art museum. She likes the museum because Mom works there. Lisa tags along when Mom tells other women why one dead painter is better than another dead painter. Lisa likes religious paintings. She likes beautiful mothers holding cute baby boys. She likes lambs and shepherds and mangers, and angels make her smile and sigh. Lisa was born in the wrong century.

I'm in my room, studying a blueprint of the space shuttle. I have a daydream about being aboard the shuttle. I'm still a kid but I win a contest. First prize is a space ride. I'm interviewed on TV and pose for pictures. Then I'm strapped in next to real astronauts and we blast off. Something happens. The astronauts pass out. *I*, with my bad sense of direction, have to land the shuttle! So I want to be ready, just in case.

There's a knock at my door. Could it be NASA already? No, it's Lisa.

"What do you want?" I snarl, putting her on the defensive.

"What are you doing? Playing?"

"Don't try to get us talking," I warn her. I know her sly trick.

"I need your help," she says.

"Me? The brother you torment? You need *my* help? These must be bad times, Lisa."

"Bernie!" She stomps her foot. She crosses her arms and sits down on my desk. I wasn't about to scare her off. "I want to go to Florida and visit Erin. You want to see the space shuttle launched at Cape Canaveral. Right?"

"Maybe." I have to be careful.

"Mom and Dad won't take us there." She looks sad. "No way. They want to buy a new water heater. Or fix the sink. Or resod the backyard. They're so selfish!"

"I'm not going to run away with you," I say.

"Thanks for nothing, you little creep!" she screams before slamming my door.

Boy, if that's what puberty is about, I never want to have it! I have a few moments of peace and quiet before Lisa reappears, wearing her coat and holding a daypack.

"I'm leaving," she announces.

"Don't forget your zit medicine," I tell her.

"I mean it this time!"

Lisa runs away about three times a month. The longest she's been gone is twenty-five minutes. She misses Mom's cooking, I guess.

"Don't forget to write," I tell her.

"Why are you such a mean kid?" she asks.

"I'm doing you a favor. The more you hate me, the better the chances that you'll finally run away to Florida and live with Erin."

She puts down her daypack. "I don't hate you. It'd be impossible around here without you. You're the only one who's honest. Mom only says 'It'll be all right, honey, don't worry.' And if Dad had to chose between the bank and us, he'd chose the bank." Without asking permission, she sits down on my bed. She slumps over like a rag doll. "We got to get away from here. A family isn't a healthy place to grow up."

"If we were famous, we wouldn't have any problems," I tell her. "Look at the people in *People* magazine. They got it made."

"Famous people have problems too," Lisa says.

"Yeah? Like what?"

"People won't leave them alone. Everyone wants to be their friend."

"I wish I had those problems." I sigh. Lisa's brushing dog hair off my bedspread. Whenever she starts acting like Mom, I know she's not going anywhere. "Anything else?" I ask.

"No," she smiles. "Thanks for listening. Guess I owe you one." She stands and straightens the books on my desk. Lisa's going to make someone a great maid someday. "I'm biking to school to practice gymnastics. Want to come?"

"No, thanks. There's something I have to do here."

Bored with space travel, bored with the encyclopedia, even bored with TV, I search my parents' room. I need to

find something to bring to school for Family Heritage
Day. Something good if I want to get an A.

Ms. Priswell has told us, "Each of your families has its
own history, its own myths and beliefs and ways of doing
things. Often an object can tell us something about its
owner. So, class, I want you to bring something from
home that can tell us about your family heritage."

Freddy Katz, always good for a laugh, raised his hand.
"We have a talking parrot, Ms. Priswell. He can repeat
what my mom and dad argue about."

Ms. Priswell nodded but did not smile. She's tired of
Freddy Katz. "Look for something old, perhaps something that belonged to your grandparents. And remember to ask your parents for permission to bring it to
school."

The only old things in our house are my parents. Cecil's
ninety-one in dog years—but will he bring me an A? No, I
need something good. Unpredictable. Awesome.

I find the path to fame in Mom's bottom drawer. Clos-
ing the drapes so the neighbors won't look in and call the
cops, I find Mom's jewelry box deep in a corner of the
drawer. I undo the lock with a hairpin—Mom should get
better protection since *I* can open it! Looking under some
necklaces she brought back from Hawaii, pushing aside a
charm bracelet, her college sorority pin, Dad's high
school ring, and a silver spoon, I see it. Resting on a bed of
velvet satin, glowing—it's a bracelet of magic coins!

I behave myself when Mom and Dad get home. Luckily, both of them have had a good day at their jobs. Even

Lisa isn't complaining. I do my part to maintain calm by—gosh!—setting the table. Mom is so pleasantly surprised she threatens to take me to the doctor. "Honey," she calls to Dad, "Bernie's helping. It's not like him—do you think he's sick?"

"Boy spends too much time in the house," Dad says. "He should be out breathing the polluted air like the rest of us."

Over a dinner of Brie burritos, tofu crepes, and Cajun pasta salad—Mom reads *Gourmet* magazine and has gone international—I bring up my life. "Tomorrow's a special day," I say. "It's Family Heritage Day. Ms. Priswell says our report will be worth five pop quizzes, two book reports, class participation, and penmanship combined. We're supposed to bring something from home." I take a big forkful of the mush on my plate, wanting Mom to think I love the meal. I have to force the stuff down and nearly throw up. I'm sweaty but smiling. "Mom, may I bring your old bracelet to school?" I ask, certain she won't mind.

"Are you crazy?" she says. "No. No, and no!"

"Why not?" I squeal.

"That bracelet is very important to me," she explains. "It's the one thing I have from my grandmother. It's very old and can't be replaced."

"That's what I tell James about you." I mean it as a joke, but Mom isn't laughing. I'm getting nowhere, so I try Dad. "Dad, I'll be careful. Tell Mom. Please." I walk over to him and put my hand on his shoulder. "James James is bringing his parents' Oklahoma football bedsheets and towels. I'll be the only kid who doesn't bring anything."

Dad looks at Mom. "Sweetie, Bernie's growing up. He needs to learn about responsibility. Let him borrow your bracelet."

Mom stares at me. "Bernard, if anything happens, you'll be grounded till you're old enough to enlist in the army. You can have the bracelet for one day. That's it." She isn't happy, but she and Dad won't argue in front of Lisa and me. They're afraid if they fight, Lisa will think they're getting a divorce.

"What could happen?" I say.

"Famous last words," Lisa mutters.

7

School is a breeze the next day. No one knocks me down during gym. The lunchroom serves barbecue beef. No one steals my food. No one pulls the chair out from under me. On the blacktop I'm actually asked to join a game of four square. Amazingly, I work my way up to become the server. I give the others my patented backspin serve, which I'd mastered alone on our back patio. No one can believe that ol' Bernard the nerdy wimp and wimpy nerd is in control.

The bell sounds and we head back inside. In Ms. Priswell's class we finish the history section about George Washington. For a week we read about Mount Vernon, Martha, the cherry tree, Valley Forge, and wooden teeth. Frankly, I know all I'd ever want to know about George Washington. Okay, he was a great man—but can you imagine him smiling?

Just before the bell, Ms. Priswell says, "As you know, tomorrow begins our study of family heritage. And I'd like a volunteer to do his or her report first."

Freddy Katz raises his hand and says, "I volunteer Bernie."

"Actually," I say, "I was going to volunteer myself." I have my hands folded on my desk. My posture is perfect, and I'm wearing the fancy sweater Grandma sent from Florida.

Ms. Priswell can tell I'm serious. "Very well, Bernie," she says, marking me down on her schedule. "You'll be first."

When I get home I discover that Mom is planning another horrible dinner. It's sitting in our microwave, on the timer. I can't face another meal at home—so I crank up the temperature to 1600 degrees, turn on the oven, and vaporize Mom's cooking. In our living room I turn on the TV and watch a few minutes of *Sesame Street* just to see what they're teaching tots nowadays. I pull down the S volume of our encyclopedia and read about Alan Shepard, my favorite old astronaut. He was the first American to be blasted into space—and he did it on the day that would later be my birthday!

Mom and Lisa come home together. When Mom asks what happened to her cooking I shrug my shoulders and say, "I don't know. It was that way when I got home. Maybe the microwave glitched. Does this mean we can go out for pizza?"

"We have guests coming for dinner," she says, upset.

"We do?"

"Daddy called from the bank. He needs to entertain a client. He won't like it, but we'll have to go to a restaurant."

And that's what happens. Lisa and I have to wear our fanciest clothes. How I hate that suit with its itchy pants! Sitting in the backseat, she and I buckle up as Dad drives to Chez Hunan, the most expensive restaurant at the mall.

"By the way," he says, glancing at me through the rearview mirror, "I think you know these people."

"Me?" I say. "Are they famous?"

"The daughter goes to your school."

"I don't know any girls," I tell them. "It's against my religion."

"No one is ever going to marry you," Lisa butts in. "Not even if you have a billion dollars and look like Michael J. Fox."

"Kids, this is an important dinner for Daddy," Mom informs us. "We need to impress our guests. So, Bernie, don't act like an idiot."

"Mr. McCoy owns the largest Toyota dealership in three states," Dad says, impressed.

"McCOY!" I yell. "Dad, stop this car!"

But it's too late. I'm having dinner with Candy McCoy. She orders something gross, like hacked chicken stomachs with lobster egg sauce. Lisa and I agree to share sweet and sour shrimp. Mr. McCoy is wearing a plaid suit. His hair is so thick and perfect that I bet it's *sewn* to his scalp. He talks about Japanese cars as though they're golden chariots from ancient Egypt. Dad slaps Mr. McCoy on the back, then orders two more beers.

Mom and Mrs. McCoy sit near Lisa, Candy, and me. Candy is praising *me*. She tells Mom, "Bernie is never late for class. He tries hard at history. Since he got glasses his reading skills have improved. . . ."

"Who is this girl?" Lisa whispers.

"Everybody hates her because she's so perfect," I whisper back.

Then Mrs. McCoy bores us with an account of her recent vacation in Europe. "All we did was spend money and eat like pigs," she chuckles.

I wish I hadn't vaporized Mom's cooking. At least if we were home I could go to my room and shut the door.

8

The next morning I spend some extra time in the bathroom. I slick down my cowlick and polish my glasses. Then I brush and floss and brush and floss my teeth. I even clip my fingernails and, just to be on the safe side, my toenails. I wear the expensive clothes Mom picked out for me at a store named Henny's Young Men's Shoppe. I put Mom's bracelet in my pocket.

During lunch, I trade James James my sack for a favor. "Please cheer when I give my report in Ms. Priswell's class," I request. "Whoop it up. You like me, right?"

"Yeah. You're okay for a wimp." He's lifting the bread from the sandwich. Mom has made me roast beef on rye, with honey, lettuce, artichoke hearts, and a Snickers bar smashed inside—my favorite. James starts to devour it.

"If you think the bracelet is great, everyone else will," I add. "Talk it up big. Please."

He shrugs, his mouth full. "Your mom packs a great lunch." He finishes the sandwich, then licks his fingers. He belches and smiles. All I have to eat is a napkin. "Isn't a bracelet a *girl's* thing?" he asks.

ELLENSVILLE ..... LIBRARY

"That's why I need your help," I tell him. "You're macho. And I can use a macho man."

"This better be good," he says.

Science is next and our teacher, Ms. Glitzer, is sick. We have a substitute who only teaches French. Since she doesn't know us, we're free to sit anywhere. And Candy McCoy sits down next to me! What does she want?

After calling roll and getting all our names wrong, the sub tells us we're seeing a movie. The lights go out. The blinds are outlined in sunlight. Then the projector sputters on, the reels start to turn and creak, and the gray screen turns white. I have the strange feeling that Candy is moving her chair nearer to mine.

The film starts and we see spotted fawns nibbling grass. A bird brings dead bugs to four hungry chicks. A baby sucks a woman's bare softie machine.

"Gross!" Freddy Katz yells.

On cue, the rest of us boys join in. "Gross! Gross! Gross!"

The lights go on. The projector sputters off. The screen turns gray again.

The sub is upset. "What's your name?" she asks Freddy.

"Biffo Whitebread," he says. We chuckle.

She checks the roll. "I don't see your name listed."

A paper missile sails overhead. Its nose rams into the blackboard.

"Give me a break, kids," the sub pleads. "Ms. Glitzer will be back tomorrow."

"Boo!" Ms. Glitzer is hard.

"QUIET! Or I'll get the principal!"

The class grows very quiet.

The lights go off again. The projector sputters on and the reels creak. On the screen a couple walks hand in hand. They sit in a fancy restaurant and drink wine. They slow dance. They walk along the shore, under moonlight. They lie near lit candles. They hug and smooch. I wonder what they're selling.

We nearly die holding in the giggles. Suddenly, near my hand I sense something warm and clammy, like a wet, cooked worm. It's Candy's hand, touching me!

I promise myself to call the doctor for a blood test.

Then the film turns into a cartoon. A circle splits into two. The twos turn into four. The fours to sixteen. And then I lose count. . . . This film is about s-e-x!

Then I feel her hand again. Slimy, like warm Jell-O. If I scream, I'll get sent to the principal. If I tell James, he'll tell everyone else that Candy touched me. Then they'll talk to me less than they do now. I swallow hard. I'm dying. And Candy is smiling.

The class before my report is music. Our teacher, Ms. Merman—who looks like a fire hydrant—is making up pairs for next week's dance festival.

"I'll pass this hat around," she tells us. "I've written the boys' names on small squares of papers. Girls, reach in, and the boy whose name you pick will be your partner. Isn't this exciting?"

I sit in the back with James James. We're bored. James is picked by Betsy Callas. He's lucky. For a girl she's not bad.

As the hat is passed, we look around to see who's left. It's

getting close. With my luck I'll end up with Candy Mc-
Coy.

Candy is not dandy. She's the worst! The pits! It's a good
thing she's in the other reading section. Otherwise we'd
have to look at her all day long. But we share books with
the other reading section, and Candy is the book monitor.

When she comes into our room to return the books, all
us boys hold our breaths. We don't want to catch anything
from her. We're sure that she has rabies or cooties or B.O.
or some other fatal disease. If you breathe when Candy
McCoy is in the room, you're a goner! But she's no
dummy. She takes her sweet time putting the books away.
Half of us boys nearly pass out.

One time she stopped on her way out to chat with Ms.
Priswell. I looked around. James James was turning blue.
Freddy Katz was choking. I snuck a couple quick breaths
through my nose, but my brain felt lighter and lighter.
Content that she had ruined our lungs, Candy finally left.
At that instant, fifteen boys let go, sending paper flying. It
was a close call.

Now there's only one girl left to reach into the hat.
Candy McCoy. And only one boy's name left. Mine! The
boys start to laugh, and James hits me in the arm. I grab
my throat, stick out my tongue, and start to gag.

Everyone turns around and sings:

> *Candy and Bernie sitting in a tree,*
> *K-I-S-S-I-N-G!*
> *First comes the ring,*

Then comes marriage,
Then comes Bernie Junior in a baby carriage!

"Class! Class! Attention!" Ms. Merman shouts. "That'll be enough."

I raise my hand. "May I be excused?" I moan. "I'm going to barf!"

"Bernard, be nice." Ms. Merman scolds. "Now, class, I'm going to play the music you'll dance to." She turns on the phonograph. It plays a silly song named "The Teddy Bears' Picnic."

While the song plays, Candy keeps looking at me. Smiling. Batting her eyelashes. Making kissy-kissing noises.

When the song ends, Ms. Merman says, "Okay, everyone find your partner. I want three lines. Boy, girl, boy, girl. Hurry!"

I drag myself off my chair and stumble toward Candy.

"Wait till my parents hear about this," she whispers.

I'd like to quit school but I don't want Dad to lose his job. Just standing next to Candy McCoy gives me the shakes. She's grinning, looking straight ahead. She knows soon she'll touch me and pass on the creeping crud or some other disease. I'm breathing through my nose.

"Now face your partner and take their hands," Ms. Merman shouts. She's always shouting. I think it was part of her voice lessons.

I take one last free breath, then face Candy. She puts out her hands. They look like squids. I close my eyes, put my hands out. She grabs them and squeezes.

"Now, put your right foot out," Ms. Merman shouts.

"Now shake your ankle. Now do the same thing with your left foot." Ms. Merman shows us. She looks like a drunken flamingo. "Raise your hands above your head and make a circle with your partner. Wonderful! Wonderful! Let go of your partner. Jump up and down three times. Pretend you're a tree shaking its leaves."

This is dancing?

"Now from the top." Ms. Merman turns on the music.

No one does the dance right, except Candy, of course. James jumps when he is supposed to go in a circle. Betsy goes in a circle when she is supposed to be a tree. I just stand there while Candy prances around like she's a belly dancer.

"No! No! No!" Ms. Merman screams. "We have only a few days to get ready. Do you want to make fools of yourselves? Why, a five-year-old could learn this dance."

"So get a five-year-old," I suggest.

"Don't get smart with me, Bernard. How would you feel if everyone *but* you performed?"

"I'd feel fine, thank you."

She storms over and stands right above me. I have to stare at her mighty bosom. "Bernard!"

I tell her I'm sorry. After all, my report is next.

"That's not true. The kings of ancient Egypt were buried wearing gold bracelets on their wrists and ankles," I inform them.

"So?" Bronto snorts, saying one of the few words he knows.

"Let me see it," James says, putting his hand out.

I take the bracelet and give it to him. While he inspects it I repeat what Mom has told me, " 'The bracelet comes from Poland, where my grandmother lived as a little girl. The coins were then used for money. Inflation made the coins worthless, so they were made into this charm bracelet, which is now worth a lot.' "

"It's kinda neat," James says. "The coins are cool. Kings and armored horses. Eagles and swords. But the chain is queer." Without asking me, he tosses the bracelet to Bronto. I hope Bronto doesn't think that it's food.

"Be careful!" I tell him slowly. I turn to James and say, "Mom will kill me if anything happens to that bracelet."

"No, she won't. Your mom's okay," James assures me.

"You don't live with her," I say. "I'm responsible for that bracelet."

"Look, she's not going to kill you," James tells me. Is he suddenly a lawyer? "The question is, Do you want a good grade or not? You know you'll probably get a B. Ms. Priswell would give you a B even if you stood on your head and spoke the Pledge of Allegiance in Polish. The only way you may get an A is if I support you. I think Ms. Priswell has the hots for my dad. But I can't support a guy who likes bracelets and knows about mummies."

"What are you suggesting?" I ask.

9

_____

After music I go to the lav. I'm starting to feel nervous. All of a sudden I'm convinced the bracelet will be a flop! I should've rehearsed a speech. Maybe I should pretend I'm sick and skip Ms. Priswell's class. I could go to the nurse, complaining of a stomachache. But any kid who goes to the nurse has to lie down and raise his or her legs into the air.

I try to pee. But even *that* isn't working! I stand at the urinal like a fool, doing nothing but holding myself.

James James and Bronto Blahberg walk in, discussing football. Bronto Blahberg has a great future with the circus. He's the biggest kid in our school. Rumor has it he shaves every day.

I zip up and motion to James James. He walks over, wiggling his shoulders. "Yeah?" he asks.

"I have to give my report when the bell rings," I tell him. "And I'm not sure what to say."

"About that bracelet of yours?" James asks. "Say you're a homo. Only girls and homos like bracelets." He turns to Bronto Blahberg and they both laugh.

Then comes marriage,
Then comes Bernie Junior in a baby carriage!

"Class! Class! Attention!" Ms. Merman shouts. "That'll be enough."

I raise my hand. "May I be excused?" I moan. "I'm going to barf!"

"Bernard, be nice." Ms. Merman scolds. "Now, class, I'm going to play the music you'll dance to." She turns on the phonograph. It plays a silly song named "The Teddy Bears' Picnic."

While the song plays, Candy keeps looking at me. Smiling. Batting her eyelashes. Making kissy-kissing noises.

When the song ends, Ms. Merman says, "Okay, everyone find your partner. I want three lines. Boy, girl, boy, girl. Hurry!"

I drag myself off my chair and stumble toward Candy.

"Wait till my parents hear about this," she whispers.

I'd like to quit school but I don't want Dad to lose his job. Just standing next to Candy McCoy gives me the shakes. She's grinning, looking straight ahead. She knows soon she'll touch me and pass on the creeping crud or some other disease. I'm breathing through my nose.

"Now face your partner and take their hands," Ms. Merman shouts. She's always shouting. I think it was part of her voice lessons.

I take one last free breath, then face Candy. She puts out her hands. They look like squids. I close my eyes, put my hands out. She grabs them and squeezes.

"Now, put your right foot out," Ms. Merman shouts.

"Now shake your ankle. Now do the same thing with your left foot." Ms. Merman shows us. She looks like a drunken flamingo. "Raise your hands above your head and make a circle with your partner. Wonderful! Wonderful! Let go of your partner. Jump up and down three times. Pretend you're a tree shaking its leaves."

This is dancing?

"Now from the top." Ms. Merman turns on the music.

No one does the dance right, except Candy, of course. James jumps when he is supposed to go in a circle. Betsy goes in a circle when she is supposed to be a tree. I just stand there while Candy prances around like she's a belly dancer.

"No! No! No!" Ms. Merman screams. "We have only a few days to get ready. Do you want to make fools of yourselves? Why, a five-year-old could learn this dance."

"So get a five-year-old," I suggest.

"Don't get smart with me, Bernard. How would you feel if everyone *but* you performed?"

"I'd feel fine, thank you."

She storms over and stands right above me. I have to stare at her mighty bosom. "Bernard!"

I tell her I'm sorry. After all, my report is next.

"Twist the coins off the chain. Pretend that there never was a bracelet. Talk about the coins. How, I don't know, some general received them as he conquered the Communists a few hundred years ago."

"James, there weren't any Communists a few hundred years ago."

He leans close and whispers, "Dad says there's always been Communists. Back then they were a secret known only to themselves."

I shake my head. "Mom will go nuts if I break her bracelet."

James takes the bracelet from Bronto and tells him to wait outside. He then turns toward me. "We're not breaking it," he says. "We'll still have the coins and the chain, only in separate places. I'll keep the chain and no one else will know. Don't worry about Bronto. He does what I tell him."

I can't decide. I need to get an A to make my parents happy, but they'll kill me if I break Mom's bracelet. If I show everyone the bracelet, James and his friends will call me a homo, and Ms. Priswell will give me a B. Is James truly my friend?

The bell rings.

"It's up to you," James says coolly. "You could tell your mom that the coins just fell off."

"*Seven* coins just fell off? Right!"

James begins to toy with the bracelet.

"Hey, be careful!" I tell him. I try to take it from him, but he turns his shoulder, knocking my hand away. "James, please!"

"Uh-ohh," I hear him say. He shrugs his shoulders and eyebrows. "The chain was weak." He holds up a coin broken off the chain.

"Great," I mutter and sigh. "Give me the bracelet, okay? We have to get to class."

"We've gone this far," he says, "why not go all the way?"

"What?"

"Might as well break all the coins off," he says. "You can't get into worse trouble than you already are, and at least you'll come home with an A."

I'm confused. Deep down I think, *Don't listen to James. He doesn't think about other people. He doesn't consider me his friend. He only bothers with me when he's not out with his jock pals. He comes over to look at Lisa, since she's suffering puberty. Would I rather do as James thinks or as I feel is right?*

My brain advises, *James has it made. Be like he is. Think how he thinks. Do you want to be a lonely outsider all your life?*

"We got to get to class," he tells me, handing back the bracelet and coin. He starts to walk off, leaving me.

"Hey, James," I call out.

"Yeah?" He turns around.

I quickly twist off the remaining coins, then toss the chain to him.

"We'll make a soldier out of you yet," he says with a grin.

Standing there, in shock, I feel nothing.

In class, Ms. Priswell smiles at me and says, "Everyone's waiting."

My head low, I trudge to the front of the room. "I brought these coins for my family heritage report." I pass them down the row. Kids inspect them, then pass them on. "I brought them because I thought they were neat," I begin. "Old coins from Poland, where my mother's grandmother came from. These coins were once worth something. Now they couldn't buy a tuna fish sandwich if your life depended on it. Any questions?"

"What do these coins mean to your family?" Ms. Priswell asks, ready to grade me.

I shrug my shoulders. "Not much, I guess. They were put away in my mom's drawer."

"Well," Ms. Priswell then says, "perhaps it's what the coins represent which is important. Is money part of your family heritage?"

I think for a moment. "My dad works in a bank. He'd be unemployed and broke without money. And my mom loves nice things. So, yeah, money's very important. It's what we usually talk about over dinner. It's what my parents fight about when they're not fighting about my sister and me."

"May I ask why money's so important?" Ms. Priswell asks.

"It's important to everyone. Without money you don't get on TV unless you're a criminal."

"But aren't there more important things than money?" Ms. Priswell asks the class.

James James raises his hand and is called. "First off, I

think Bernie's coins are great and deserve the highest grade. Second, yeah, being famous is more important than money. But if you're famous you have money and the other way around. I mean, name me a poor president or top jock."

Ms. Priswell then calls on Freddy Katz.

"James is right," Freddy adds. "Money and fame are in first place. Everything else is far behind."

"Class, I'm disappointed," Ms. Priswell says. "There are things in life much more important than fame and money. Things like love and being a good person, for instance. Or helping others and being generous." She turns to me and asks, "Am I right?"

Knowing my grade depends on my answer, I say, "You're absolutely right, Ms. Priswell. Love, respecting others, telling the truth—all these things are more important than fame and money."

Ms. Priswell smiles. "Thank you, Bernie, for an interesting report. Do you want me to announce your grade?"

I nod.

"B," she tells me.

I glance at James James, who can only shrug his shoulders.

10

"I broke Mom's bracelet!" I moan on the way home from school. My knees become weak.

"You shouldn't have done it," James says, walking with me. "You're in hot water now."

"But you made me! You dared me!"

"Hey, you're not dragging me into this mess," James says.

"What am I going to do?"

"Just don't mention the bracelet," James advises. "Your mom will forget she ever lent it to you."

"Are you kidding? The first thing she'll ask is 'Where's my bracelet?' "

"Tell her you were robbed."

"She'll never believe that."

"Then tell her the truth," James suggests. "When you took the bracelet from your pocket, the coins were snapped off the chain."

"That's not the truth," I tell him.

"Yes, but she doesn't know that." He punches me in the

arm. "Keep cool. Lighten up and tighten up. Be the master of disaster."

We reach his house. "I have to try to fix it," I tell him. "Do you have any glue?"

"We sure do. All types of glue."

We go to his dad's workbench and try all types of glue, but none of them works. "I'm a dead duck," I moan.

"Just return the coins to her jewelry box," he advises. "And don't say a word. I'll hold on to the chain and show it to Dad when he comes home. I bet he'll know what to do. Any problem, call me."

"James, you're true blue," I say.

We shake hands, then I go home to face the music.

In my room I practice pleas for mercy:

"Mom. Remember that old bracelet? The one that was ready to fall apart? Remember how beat-up it looked? Well, it finally broke. It was an accident. No one's to blame. Luckily, no one got hurt. . . ."

"Mom. Remember when I told you that Bronto Blahberg was bothering me? Remember how big and awful I said he was? Well, today after school, he pinned me down. I tried to fight back, honest I did. But he reached into my pocket and broke your bracelet! The filthy swine . . ."

"Bandits, Mom. Horrible masked men knocked me down and tried to steal your bracelet. I fought like crazy, and I was able to rescue the coins. . . ."

No, it's no use. I'm a goner!

Dinner is quiet. Lisa doesn't say much and neither do I.

Dad winks at Mom. "Honey, this meal is delicious. Much better than eating out!"

I hardly eat my food. My stomach is twisted and hurts. Time crawls. Somehow we reach dessert without Mom asking me about the bracelet.

Lisa keeps looking at me. We're almost finished with dinner, and I start to think that maybe I'll get away with it!

Then Mom pushes her chair back. She stands, leans toward me to take my plate, and smiles. "Oh, by the way, how was your report?"

I start to choke, to cough. I can't remember a single plea for mercy.

"Bernie, your mother asked you a question," Dad says.

My brain is a clean slate. I reach into my pocket and feel the coins, curling my fingers around them. I take my hand out and slowly open my fingers.

Mom studies my palm. "Those are only the coins. Where's the gold chain?"

I swallow. "GOLD? James has it."

"Mom, if you and Dad weren't so . . ." Lisa starts to say.

"Quiet, please. This doesn't concern you," Mom tells her. She turns to me. Her eyebrow is quivering. "Why does James have the chain?"

"He's keeping it."

Mom put the dishes down. "Bernard!"

"Oh, Mom, the bracelet broke at school," I said. "One of the coins broke right before my report. And . . ."

"Better tell the truth," Dad interrupts.

My shoulders sag, then I start to cry. Mom and Dad become angry blurs. "I did it. I snapped the coins off because James made me. I wasn't thinking. Mom, I didn't know the chain was gold. Honest. Don't break my face."

She looks at Dad. Dad looks at Lisa. Lisa looks at me. I look at Dad. He looks at Mom. She looks at me.

"Why does James have the chain?" Dad asks.

"Because he wants to fix it. Honest. And he says his dad will know how."

Mom hits her head with her hand. "Bernie, what is wrong with you? Call James and get the chain back. We'll deal with what you did afterwards." She is burning laser rays through me. She is too angry to scream. I've really done it this time.

I push back my chair, praying silently to James. *Don't let me down.* Everyone but Cecil follows me into the kitchen. Sensing trouble, Cecil crouches by the front door. I dial James's phone number and he answers.

"James, they know everything," I tell him.

"You dope!"

"Did your dad find a way to fix the bracelet?"

"Well, not exactly."

"Why not?" I ask. Mom is breathing hot air on my head.

"Bernie, listen," James whispers. "When Mom came home she got mad because my room was messy."

"So?"

Dad glances around the kitchen. Is he looking for a pan to belt me with?

"She was on a terror, understand?" James says. "Cleaning my room from top to bottom. I knew if she found the chain she'd start asking questions—maybe kick me out of football. I'd be ruined before Dad came home to save me."

"So?"

Lisa was creeping back into the other room, no doubt planning her own escape.

"I had to destroy the evidence," James says. "Like spies do. I flushed the chain down the toilet."

"What?" I scream.

"What?" Dad asks, shaking me.

"What?" Mom adds, shaking Dad.

"James, that chain was *gold.*"

"Really?" he says. "Uh-oh. Bernie, I'm sorry. But don't drag me into this or I'll murder you."

"Don't worry," I tell him. "My parents will beat you to it." I hang up the phone. I press my chin into my stomach and mumble, "He flushed the chain down the toilet."

Mom starts to rumble like a volcano. "Go to your room! You've done it this time, Bernard!"

I slink out like a drowned worm.

11

I'm in my room, stir-crazy. I can't go out, except to the bathroom. The rest of the house belongs to Mom. I'm about to climb the walls. I don't bother with homework. "Why do homework," I ask myself, "if I'll be dead tomorrow anyway?" I can't play my radio. After all, I'm supposed to be in here *thinking,* not having a good time. Dad calls this form of punishment "stewing in one's juices."

So I'm thinking about my juices, about the bad boy I must be. I always had doubts about my appearance. I don't like my height—or lack of it. I think my hair is worthless. I'm only cute when I smile. And I try not to smile, because my teeth aren't straight. Now I have new doubts, thanks to that stupid bracelet of coins! Tears collect on my eyeglasses. I'm sobbing like a baby.

I haven't felt this bad since the time I broke Dad's digital alarm clock. He nearly killed me. He loved that clock because a voice, not a bell, woke him up. "It's seven A.M.," the tinny robot tone would announce. "Time to get up." Dad loves gadgets.

I was trying to sneak outside one night. My usual route

was blocked because the kitchen was being remodeled. I wanted to be outside with the night sky, and I wasn't sleepy. There was time for a quick stare into space. But the only other door to the backyard was in my parents' room.

I was doing quite well. I had snuck by their bed and disarmed the security system. Just when I was reaching for the door to the backyard, Mom woke up. "Oh, my God!" she screamed. "There's someone in our room!"

Dad woke up, groggy but in command. "Honey, call the police," he ordered Mom, "and I'll fight him off!"

"Mom! Dad!" I yelled. "It's me! Bernie. Your only son. Don't shoot!"

"Bernie!" Mom pulled the blanket up to her chin. "You frightened us! What are you doing in here?"

"What are you frightened of?" I asked her.

Dad rolled over and chuckled. "Crime's out there, son. Danger. Our fearless leaders. War. Poverty. Pollution. Cancer. Ruin."

"Shhh," Mom told him. "You'll frighten Bernie."

"There's nothing bad outside in the dark," I told them. "Especially if the night's clear so starlight shines through. Grab a robe and come with me."

"Bernie, are you feeling well?" Mom asked. She opened her arms. "Come here. Let me feel your head."

I had no choice, so I moved toward the bed. But I tripped over Dad's running shoes, fell, and landed right on top of him. He sat up with a howl and knocked me off. I flew off the bed and broke his alarm clock.

I thought he'd murder me on the spot. "Bernie!" he

moaned, doubled over. I got up and raced to Mom. I quickly pressed my forehead to her cheek. Her skin was warm.

"Go back to bed," she said, saving me. "You're cool as a cucumber."

"Is that good?" I asked. She nodded. Her face was puffy. Not waiting to hear from Dad, I went back to my room and climbed into bed. I put the blanket over my head after putting a few essentials on the mattress: a flashlight, a model of the space shuttle, and my slippers.

I sat up, the blanket crowning my head. The flashlight became the sun. I steered the shuttle toward the light— and beyond. I soared in curved space, safe in my house.

But that time was different. Dad's clock could be replaced, and it hadn't belonged to his grandmother. It was an accident—I wasn't to blame. I didn't hurt anyone's feelings. Feelings stay hurt longer than a scrape or bruise.

I get undressed, put on my pajamas, and sneak into the bathroom. I try not to look at myself in the mirror. Who wants to see a sorry-looking jerk? The tile floor is like an iceberg under my toes.

I return to my room and flop on the bed. My room feels a billion miles away from the rest of the house. I can't sleep.

After dark, after everyone else has gone to bed, I sneak outside. I need to be with the stars. Lying down on the cool lawn, I try to fall into the sky. I want to float away, but I can't. I'm not going anywhere. I'm as heavy as the earth.

I go into the kitchen to get a glass of milk, and sit in the dark. I've cried so much I can't cry anymore. Still, I feel awful. If I were my parents, I'd hate me. The milk tastes like Elmer's Glue.

Then Lisa and Cecil walk in. "I heard you out here whimpering," she tells me. "We should run away. We should go to Florida and never return."

"What do they have planned for me?" I ask.

"They're still considering what to do," she says. "Mom wants to really give it to you, but Dad is trying to calm her down."

I pour out the milk and put the glass in the sink. "I can't stand this. I'm going in there."

"Into their room?" Lisa asks, wide-eyed. "Are you crazy?"

"Probably."

I walk through the house. I tap lightly on their door, then enter. Mom and Dad are in bed and the TV is on, glowing like a fire in a cave. The air is so stuffy I can barely breathe.

Mom doesn't move her eyes from the TV. "I'm too angry to talk with you now, Bernard. You hurt me very deeply."

I look down. "I kno-o-o-o-ow!"

Dad punches his pillow, trying to sleep.

"What are you going to do to me?" I ask.

"For starters—you're out of the dance festival!"

"Just because Bernie's a jerk is no reason to punish his class," Dad mutters, his eyes closed. "I'm certain Ms. Merman will have problems if he doesn't take part."

"Is this right?" Mom asks m[...] out of the dance festival?"

I nod. "Mom, believe me, y[...] if I have to dance with Can[...]

She continues to stare a[...] grounded for three weeks. [...] sleep-overs. No bike trips t[...]

"Okay." I leave them. I'v[...] No violence. No chains, w[...] word. Mom and Dad are t[...] even if they hate me.

12

The story of the bracelet is all over school. My *good friend* James tells Freddy who tells Bronto who tells Candy who tells Betsy who tells . . . Well, you get the idea.

Worse yet, I tell Bronto Blahberg to shut up. I lost my head. Now I'm going to lose my life.

Bronto provoked me. At lunch he called me a moron. He shot his straw wrapper at me. He stole my brownie. He drooled into my chili. "Bernie's in trouble," he sang.

"Shut up, Brontosaurus!" I shouted. It slipped out.

I look at James. He will protect and save me. But he picks up his tray and walks off.

Bronto leans across the table, smashing my hamburger with his fist. "What did you say?"

"Did I say anything? I didn't say anything."

"Yes, you did. I heard you," Bronto growls. "My hearing is as good as a bat's."

And you look like one, too, I think. "Maybe I suggested that you be quiet. That you seal your lips. Zip your teeth together. Clam up. Drain the word swamp. Bolt the vocal door. Still your tongue. Speak not. Mind your own bees-

wax. Pick on someone your own size. Or, better, pick on *something* your own size. I think there's a bus outside." I'm hoping to overload his pea brain. "Get my drift, pizza face?"

I can see his mental clogs creep forward. He picks up my smashed hamburger and eats it. I wasn't hungry anyway. "Okay," he growls between chomps. "I'll get you after school." A pickle slice flies from his mouth like a missile. "You're cruising for a bruising. You messed with the rest, now mess with the best. See you later. Say your prayers, moron!"

All afternoon I pray lightning will strike Bronto Blahberg. But it's a clear day. Not a cloud in sight. Miracles are in short order.

James nudges me during math. "Did you get in trouble last night?" he whispers.

"Is the Pope a Catholic?" I respond. "Do fish pee in the sea? Will Bronto turn me into link sausage after school?"

"Guess I wasn't thinking right when I flushed the chain down the toilet," he whispers.

"A lot of dumb thinking going around," I say. "Stupidity is contagious." We have to be quiet because the teacher is looking our way.

I pay attention until the teacher looks away. Then I ask James. "Will you help me after school? Please. I can't face Bronto by myself."

James shrugs. "Sorry, no. I can't afford to. I'm in trouble myself. My folks think you're a bad influence."

"Didn't you tell them the truth?" I whisper.

James looks ahead, like he didn't hear me.

I'll have to face Bronto by myself. I might survive—with a great plan. All day I think of nothing else, but I can't come up with a way out. My brain is on vacation and not writing postcards.

When the final bell rings I stay at my desk. My legs don't move.

"It's time to leave," Ms. Priswell tells me.

I stand up and collect my books. Stiff-legged, I head for the door. "It's been nice knowing you," I tell her.

I look down the hall. Bronto is nowhere in sight. Maybe he forgot he's promised to scramble my face.

"Here goes nothing," I say to myself and race down the hall. I hit the front doors and sprint for the bike racks. My plan is to jump on my bike, zoom off, and make my escape. But my bike is missing!

"Hello, Bernard," Bronto says, standing where my bike should be. He squeezes my arm like it's made of grapes, and drags me off toward the high-jump area. A bunch of kids are waiting at the sandpit. They never miss one of Bronto's fights.

He lets go of my arm. "I'll set the bar at two feet," he says. "Clear it and I'll tell you where your bike is. Don't clear it and I mash your face."

"You're a sport!" I move back to get a running start. I try to see myself sail over the bar. Falling into the sky, flying.

I start my approach. Fly, I think, fly!

I hit the takeoff line, going great guns. I leap up and soar into the air. I look down to see the bar below me. I'm

Superman! Han Solo! Captain Kirk! E.T.! Bim, the space walker!

Then I land in the sand, hitting something hard and painful. Metal. It hurts, like I've been stabbed. I roll over and cry out, and everyone starts to laugh.

"Find your bike?" Bronto asks.

I push some of the sand away. Yes, I'd landed on my handlebars.

"Bronto, you're nothing but a big ugly stupid turd!" I scream. Not a bright thing to say, I immediately realize.

He pulls me to my feet. He's about to smash my face. I see him pull his arm back and tighten his fist.

"Don't you dare hit my brother!" Lisa shouts, pushing her way through the crowd.

"Who's going to stop me?" Bronto asks.

"You hit Bernie and I'll call the police," Lisa tells him. Her hands are on her hips. She means what she says.

"You're just a silly girl! You won't do anything!"

Without warning, Lisa kicks Bronto between his legs. Mom had taught her how to fight off creeps. She then karate-chops his neck.

Bronto doubles over and moans, "Next time, Bernie, I'll get you alone."

"No hurry," I tell him.

Bronto and his gang leave, no doubt to set fires or something.

"Thanks," I tell Lisa.

"You got enough problems without having a hamburger as a face," she says. "Besides, you're my only brother."

We wait for a few minutes, not talking. I'm trying to

decide why she helped me. I have no idea. "Okay, I give up," I tell her. "What do you want?"

"Nothing."

"Nothing?"

"James James stopped me in the hall. He said his dad told him not to see us ever again. Mr. James thinks we're bad eggs. So I figured you could use a new friend."

"But you're my sister."

"Exactly." She helps me dig out my bike and we start for home. Neither of us is in a hurry to get there, but where else is there to go?

"When Mom and Dad get a divorce, let's go live with Grandma and Grandpa in Florida," she says. "That way I'll be near Erin. And you can see blast-offs whenever you want. You and I have to stick together. Watch out for each other. Okay?" She reaches up and pulls some dead leaves from a tree.

13

The house seems sad. The curtains are closed. The living room is too quiet. There are dirty dishes in the kitchen sink, and butter was left on the table.

Dad comes home first. That's a bad sign. It means Mom is in no hurry to see me. It means she is at the store or having her hair cut. She'd rather pick up the dry cleaning than see me.

Dad finds me in my room. "Come on," he tells me. "You stay here much longer and you'll mold. Let's clean up the kitchen. Surprise your mom. Then we can play some ball."

I follow him down the hall. In the kitchen he rinses dishes while I load the dishwasher. He sweeps and I hold the dustpan. I put the melted butter back into the refrigerator. He wipes the table with a sponge.

"Is Mom still mad at me?" I ask.

"She's upset, yes," he says. "Son, it's been a hard time recently. Mom has a lot of pressure at the museum. There's a new group of volunteers that she must train. We had to replace the furnace and buy snow tires for the cars.

We're worried about Lisa. Mom and I thought you were the least of our concerns. Then you pulled that stupid stunt with her bracelet. So now we're worried about you."

"You mean Mom doesn't hate me?"

"Parents do not hate their children—or something is very wrong. We love you and Lisa. Sometimes you hurt us. But we're not going to trade you in for a newer model. No one's perfect—not even Mom or me!" He chuckles. "But just because Mom loves you doesn't mean she can forgive you right away. She can't pretend you didn't destroy something of value. That bracelet was special because it had been in Mom's family for a long time. And the chain was gold—which you don't give to a friend to flush down the toilet. Understand?"

I empty the dustpan into the trash basket. "Yes. Dad, I feel awful. Honest. I know I did something stupid and wrong. Do you think Mom will believe me if I tell her I'm sorry?"

He opens the curtains, allowing sunlight in. "When she's ready, yes, she'll believe you."

"When will she be ready?"

"Tonight, knowing her," he says. "Mom doesn't stay upset for long. A good thing, too. Because I've done some thoughtless things to her myself." He puts the broom away. "Now, how about some ball?"

Dad and I stand at opposite ends of the backyard. He throws the football at me. I run around as it hurls through space. I look up to see it crashing toward me. Being quick of foot, I step aside as it hits the ground.

Picking up the ball, I kick it as hard as I can. It sails off

my foot and lands in front of me. "Dad, since we're buddies, can I ask you something?"

"Sure, son."

"Could you pay some attention to Lisa? She's lonely,
now that Erin is gone. And she's frightened that Mom and
you are getting a divorce."

"No one's getting a divorce. Don't talk silly," Dad says.
"Come on, toss me the ball."

I throw the ball near him. He leaps up, trying to catch it,
and comes down holding his back. "Game's over, son." He
puts his arm around me and we go inside.

In the kitchen he pours himself a glass of water. "You're
right, son," he tells me. "It's time I pay some attention to
Lisa. Maybe she and I can go away together."

"But, Dad, you promised me a trip," I remind him.

He gulps down the water. He's sweating the way
grown-ups sweat. Sweat runs down his face, and his chest
and back are wet. His hair is out of place—I can see his
bald spot.

"I'm going away soon," Dad says. "And we can afford
for me to take only one of you kids with me. We'll have to
flip a coin—to determine whether I take Lisa or you."

"Where are you going?" I ask.

"Well, I'd rather not say at the moment. Some details
still have to be worked out." Dad rinses out the glass and
dries his hands. "My back is killing me. I'm going to take a
hot bath." He pats me on my head. "Thanks for the exer-
cise, son."

To impress Mom, I clean up my room. I pile the maga-

zines in the living room into a neat stack. I brush Cecil.
Then I grab a rake and go out front.

When she steers her car into the driveway, I'm busy
raking leaves. She turns off the engine and rubs her eyes.
She can't believe what she is seeing. Usually she has to
scream fifty times for me to do anything.

"Hi, Mom," I say, laying the rake down. I rush to the car
to help carry the packages inside. "How was your day?" I
ask. "What's new? Dad and I had a great time playing
ball."

"Where is he?"

"He hurt his back again. He's in the tub."

"Not again!"

She hands me a sack of groceries. It weighs a ton but I
don't complain. I lug it inside. With a supreme effort I lift
it onto the counter, then I have to rest.

Mom enters. "Who cleaned up?" she asks.

"Dad and I."

She smiles. "Thank you." She doesn't seem upset.
Maybe I caught her by surprise.

She starts to put things away. "Where's Lisa?"

"At Karen Hornby's."

"I didn't know they were friends," Mom says.

"They're not," I tell her, getting up. "Lisa was afraid to
stay home because she's afraid you're going to murder
me."

"Lisa's being silly," Mom says.

I open the refrigerator to transfer eggs from the store
carton to the rack inside. Mom bought soda and mara-
schino cherries, so she must be ready to forgive me. I put

the milk away and close the door. "Mom, may I tell you
something?"

"What is it?"

I'm nervous for a second. What if I upset her again?
"Mom," I finally say. "I'm sorry." I feel hot and my heart is
pounding. I'm looking near her, not at her. "I'm so lucky
that you're my mom and Dad's my dad and Lisa's my
sister."

She bends down and hugs me. "Thank you, Bernie."
She rubs my hair. "Now phone Karen's house and ask Lisa
to come home."

14

The afternoon of the dance festival we have a perfect run-through. Ms. Merman is happy. "Class. Class. I'm speechless. Absolutely speechless," she says. This is a first. "You've all worked hard. Long hours. I'm proud of each and every one of you. I've never had a class like yours in all my years . . ." And she goes on for twenty minutes. If she hadn't become speechless, we might have been there all night.

I pick up my jacket and head out. I'm used to walking home alone. James doesn't even talk to me at school. Some friend he turned out to be. I walk slowly. Since I don't have any company, I see more things.

I notice the differences in houses. The gardens. The trees. The windows and roofs. I listen to different sounds. Traffic. Dogs. Radios and TVs coming from houses. The wind blowing leaves across the road.

I'm no further than a block from school when I hear my name being called. "Bernie! Wait for me!" It's Candy, who skips toward me, looking happy: hair bouncing, arms swaying, shoes clicking against the sidewalk. Maybe her mom puts something funny in her lunch.

"Bernie, you left so quickly," she says, breathless. "I wanted to walk with you."

I kick the ground and shrug my shoulders. "Oh."

"What's the matter?"

"My get up and go has gone up and went," I tell her.

"So you've had a few bad days. It happens."

"James James never has a bad day."

"Who cares about him? He's a silly boy. He's the worst dancer in the class," she says. "Worse than Freddy. Even worse than Bronto."

I look at her. She's being serious.

"We're the best," she tells me. "We dance with soul." Smiling, she reaches for my hand.

I smile back. Our hands meet. Our fingers line up, then cross. Our palms push against each other. Her flesh is warm. Her hand doesn't feel like a lobster claw, like it used to do.

Magic makes a comeback. My brain leaps into color. We walk along, holding hands. I know it sounds gross but it isn't. Luckily, no one sees us. I have enough troubles without explaining why I'm holding Candy's hand.

"I like you in glasses," she adds. "They make you look smart. I like boys to be smart and clever."

Then I stop and pull free. "Why are you doing this?" I ask her.

"Because I like you. Is that all right?"

"How could you like me?" Honest, I was curious.

"It's hard, I admit," she says with a smile.

"Are you desperate?"

"Maybe."

"Candy, come on. You can't like a nobody like me."

"You're not a nobody. So maybe you're not that cute. Maybe you're short and wear glasses. Maybe you try too hard to be funny, to be liked."

"Thanks a lot."

"Bernie, being popular isn't everything. No one's popular forever. But if you're a good person, people remember that for a long, long time. Try doing something nice for someone else, and see how good it makes you feel."

To show her I'm a sport I walk her home even though I have to go to the bathroom.

That night the school parking lot is filled with station wagons and small foreign cars. I leave my family and go backstage. I find Freddy, James, and Bronto.

The girls are in the lav, playing with make up, giggling, and talking about their hair.

"What are we supposed to be doing?" I ask Freddy.

"Putting on our costumes."

"Where are they?"

"They haven't arrived yet," he tells me. "Ms. Merman is having a nervous breakdown."

The costumes do not arrive until ten minutes before curtain time.

Poor Ms. Merman. She races around pinning up costumes. Then she shows us the dance steps for the last time. After peeking through the curtains to see that every seat is taken, she sets the lights and finds an extension cord for the phonograph.

The costumes are dumb: big floppy striped pajamas large enough for an elephant. I roll the bottoms up and they still fall over my toes. The sleeves reach to the floor. I look like I've eaten shrinking pills.

I show my costume to Ms. Merman, but she just shakes her head. "There's nothing I can do. It's too late. Just keep your stomach out or the bottoms will fall down."

"Great!" I say. "Can't you pin it?"

"I used the last pins on James's costume," she replies. Then she calls us together.

"Ouch!" James screams, sitting on a pin.

"In a moment the curtains will part," Ms. Merman tells us. "You will go out and perform. I know you're nervous. I'm nervous and I'm not dancing." She closes her eyes. "You're going out there as nobodies, but inside every one of you beats the heart of an entertainer."

I whisper to Candy, "Ms. Merman has lost her marbles."

"Break a leg," Ms. Merman shouts, near tears. "Good luck."

"She has a few screws loose," I tell Candy.

"What comes after we put our hands in the air?" Bronto asks.

Ms. Merman rolls her eyes. "Go in a circle." She rubs her forehead.

We take our places on stage. The curtains part, and the audience starts to clap, even though we haven't done a thing. Parents stand and take flash pictures. My eyes are blinded by bolts of light.

"There's James. Smile, James boy!" his father yells, pounding his hands together.

Lisa yells out, "Bernie, you look like a nerd!"

Ms. Merman puts the needle down on her scratched-up record of "The Teddy Bears' Picnic." Over the speakers the song sounds like a bunch of bears growling instead of going on a picnic.

We wait for her signal. After the song starts, she counts down on her fingers while mouthing "Five . . . four . . . three . . . two . . . one . . . GO!"

We are so nervous that everyone forgets what to do. James flexes his muscles while Betsy puts her wrong foot out. Freddy makes a circle when he's supposed to put his hands overhead. Bronto doesn't move. Only Candy and I do it right. We put our right feet out. We shake our ankles.

The audience claps along with the music. Maybe Ms. Merman paid people to be nice. She stands in the wings, singing along, doing the steps. I think she needs a long vacation somewhere quiet.

Then I look down. The bottoms of my pajamas have started to unroll. I'm dragging the baggy pants around my feet like tails. When it's time to jump up and down three times, I go up all right. But when I land I nearly slip. I put my hands above my head and jump again. This time, when I come down, I land on the bottoms. I lose my balance and slip across the stage. I slide into Betsy and knock her flat. The audience laughs and claps.

Then I try to regain my balance. But I slip again, knocking James into Bronto. They go flying. The pins in James's costume come undone, and Bronto steps on one of the

pins and screams. He jumps around, holding his foot. Betsy gets mad and pushes Bronto down, shouting "Watch out, buster!"

I glance at Ms. Merman. She's covered her face.

I try one last time to regain my balance. I'm fine until Freddy crashes into me, sending me flying. I collide with Ms. Merman and knock the phonograph over. A giant SCREEEEEEEECH whines over the speakers.

Ms. Merman grabs me. "I ought to strangle you!" she screams.

But the audience is going bonkers! They're laughing. They're clapping. They're stamping their feet. They're yelling, "MORE!" "BRAVO! BRAVO!" "ENCORE!" "YES YES YES!"

Ms. Merman removes her hands from my neck. "We're a success! They think we planned the whole thing. Bernie, go out and take a bow."

I scramble to my feet and take a few running steps, then slide all the way across the stage to Candy. I take her hand. We bow ten times before she drags me off.

Applause rumbles inside my ears. It sounds like rocket engines.

15

We're the hit of the school! The principal comes back-stage. Shaking my hand, she tells me I have a real future ahead of me. I nod politely.

Mom, Dad, and Lisa find me in the hall. "This is my girlfriend," I tell them, hugging Candy.

"Really?" Dad grins. "When are you two getting married?"

I look at Candy and smile. "We're not in any hurry."

I go into the bathroom to take off my costume.

"Hey, Bernie, guess what?" James says, as he comes in. "I can see you again. Dad just told me. We can be buddies again."

I'm not so sure I want him back. He pulls a football jersey on. It has the number one on both the front and back. Then he stands in front of the mirror and combs his hair. I think about borrowing his comb, but my hair looks fine.

"I want to walk to and from school with Candy now," I tell him on my way out.

Everyone is smiling—the festival is a big success. I look around for Candy, and find her with her parents and grandmother. Candy introduces me.

"So you're Candy's new friend," her grandmother says.

"Yes, ma'am," I say.

"Your parents should be very proud of you," Candy's dad says. "Tell your dad that I'll call him tomorrow at the bank. He and I have some business to discuss."

"Okay, Mr. McCoy." I motion Candy close, and whisper, "Want me to pick you up tomorrow morning? We can walk to school together."

"Yes," she says. "That would be wonderful." Before I can do anything she kisses me on the cheek. "Good night," she says, before leaving with her family.

My face is still red—I'm blushing like a big beet—as I find my family talking with Ms. Merman. Her arms are full of pajamas. Dad shakes my hand, then musses my hair. Mom smiles at me, and Lisa gives me a punch in the arm.

"Are there more at home like Bernie?" Ms. Merman asks my parents.

Dad chuckles. "We can't afford any more! No, Bernie's the last of his kind. After him, we broke the mold."

"Thanks a lot," I say.

When we start for home, I walk ahead with Mom. Lisa and Dad are behind us. He has his arm around her, and she's happy.

At home, it's dark. The house is cold. The new furnace is broken. A repair person could come tonight but would be expensive. And, you know, money doesn't grow on trees. So we'll wait until tomorrow for heat.

Mom dishes out ice cream for all of us. We finish all the ice cream in the freezer, and my stomach is nearly frozen. It might seem weird to eat ice cream in a cold house, but then we all like ice cream. Lisa puts the empty bowls on the floor, so Cecil can lick them clean.

Before we leave the kitchen, Dad takes a coin from his pocket.

"It looks like I'll be going away," he says. "The bank wants me to go to Florida, and I want to take one of you kids with me. Flipping a coin seems as good as any other method."

"No!" Lisa screams.

"Lisa, honey, what's the matter?" Mom says.

"I don't want the family to break up. Please." Lisa is upset, she's crying like a sprinkler system. "It's not fair. Just because everyone else is getting divorced doesn't mean you have to, too!"

"Oh, Lisa," Mom says, taking Lisa in her arms. "Daddy and I are very happy together."

"But you fight."

"On occasion," Mom tells her. "Sure. Disagreeing on certain things is part of living together. But Dad and I always forgive each other. We understand that getting mad and making up are part of life. Look at Bernie—"

"What?" I interrupt. "I didn't do anything!"

"Look at Bernie," Mom starts again. "He did something hurtful, breaking my bracelet, and I got mad. But he told me he was sorry and I forgave him because I love him, as I love you, Lisa. If you love someone, the forgiving part is easy. People aren't perfect. We all make mistakes."

"Hey, we're all in this together," Dad adds.

"I'm glad you're not getting divorced," Lisa says. "But I wish you hadn't kept Dad's trip a secret. Because I got confused, and scared."

Mom and Dad look at each other.

"You're absolutely right," Dad tells Lisa. "See, even parents make mistakes!"

"I could've told you that!" I say. Then I add, "Just kidding," so Mom and Dad won't get angry.

"Okay, now are you ready for the coin toss?" Dad asks. "Here's the deal. I'm going down to Florida around Christmas. Since school will be on vacation, Mom and I thought one of you kids could come along. We can visit Grandpa and Grandma—"

"I could visit Erin!" Lisa interrupts.

"I could visit Cape Canaveral!" I say, louder than Lisa. "Maybe there'll be a shuttle lift-off to watch!"

"Okay, okay, calm down," Dad says. "Ready?"

Lisa and I nod.

Dad tosses the coin high in the air. "Call it, Bernie," he says.

"Heads!" I shout.

The coin reaches the top of its flight, then, spinning, drops toward the ground. It lands on the floor and twirls like a top before falling flat.

Lisa and I run to it. "Heads!" I announce. "It's heads!"

"Two out of three?" Lisa asks me.

"No way! I won! I won!" I jump up and do a quick

boogaloo, moon-walking across the linoleum floor. I snap my fingers and wiggle my hips. I pump my arms in the air.

"Bernie, be a good winner," Dad says. "You're making Lisa feel bad."

I stop my celebration, and shrug. "Sorry. I just got excited, that's all."

"Come on, kids," Mom says. "How about if we all climb into the big bed and watch some TV."

After putting on pajamas and brushing our teeth, Lisa and I—and Cecil—get in the big bed in my parents' room. Dad pulls the TV close so we all can see. If there were a refrigerator nearby, we'd never have to leave the bed.

Lisa leans over and pats me on the back. "I'm happy for you, Bernie," she says. "I hope you have the best time in Florida."

"Thanks." I start to think what I'll pack. I'll need warm clothes in case there's a blast-off to attend. What if one of the astronauts becomes sick and can't go? What if NASA spots me in the crowd and decides that I'd make the perfect replacement? What if I'm able to blast off with the shuttle? Gosh! I'd better pack some extra underwear and a pair of pliers.

"Don't cry," Mom tells Lisa, who is all upset. "Next time you can go with Dad."

"Bernie won fair and square," Dad adds.

"I know," Lisa whimpers.

Then it hits me. If *she* were going, she could visit Erin. They could be together and tell secrets again. Now they have to wait for months and months. Seeing Erin would make Lisa happier than anything else.

"Can I ask one favor?" I ask Mom and Dad. "About Florida."

"Yes."

"Let Lisa go, instead of me." I shrug my shoulders. "I can watch the shuttle on TV. Besides, if I go when it's warmer I can work on my tan."

"Are you sure, son?" Dad asks.

"Bernie, are you feeling all right?" Mom asks.

I nod. "I want Lisa to go."

Mom and Dad smile.

Lisa gets me in a handlock and starts to kiss me.

"Stop it!" I warn her, "or I'll change my mind!"

I wait for everyone else to fall asleep. Dad and Cecil are first. They put their heads down and they're out cold. I touch Dad's nose: it feels like a cherry popsicle. Mom's next. She rolls on her side and snuggles next to Dad. When she starts to purr, I know she's in dreamland. Lisa's last. She's so excited about going to Florida that she runs to the bathroom three times before she nods off. She falls asleep against Mom's legs. There's not much room left. I'm curled like a rope in the corner of the bed.

I wait a few minutes more, listening to the snores and purrs and puttering. Sleeping people crack me up! They look so helpless and sound like sloppy motors. I wait a little longer. Then I disarm the security system, sneak out, and put on my parka and boots.

I creep through the freezing house. In the kitchen I

open the fridge door for light. The food inside the fridge is warmer than I am. I take a sip of juice, then slide the porch door open. I put on my mittens, and stepping out, walk across the cold lawn. My boots leave prints in the frost. The grass is frozen stiff. Maybe it's this cold in space. My teeth start to chatter. I decide to stay outside for only a minute. No reason to become *really* sick.

I lie on my back. My knees are shaking. Above me the sky is clear, shiny with stars. Taking off my glasses, I close my eyes and think about falling into the sky. I don't need the shuttle to fly. It's just some machine. I'll use my own power instead.

I feel the ground start to shake. Mighty rocket engines roar in my throat, and my head becomes light as air. My body is suddenly warm. There is nothing but clear sky ahead. I'm ready. All systems go. At any moment I may blast off.

About the Author

LARRY BOGRAD's most recent book for Delacorte Press was *Poor Gertie*. The author of numerous books for children and young adults, he also writes fiction, plays, and screenplays for adults. He divides his time between New York City and Denver, Colorado.

About the Illustrator

RICHARD LAUTER has illustrated many books for children. He lives in New Jersey.